D0587250

This book belongs to:

_____

5430000045529 4

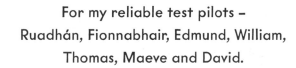

For my reliable test pilots –
Ruadhán, Fionnabhair, Edmund, William,
Thomas, Maeve and David.

Other books by Chris Judge

THE LONELY BEAST

THE BRAVE BEAST

THE GREAT EXPLORER

**Bracknell Forest
Borough Council**

5430000045529 4	
Askews & Holts	2015

This paperback edition first published in 2015 by Andersen Press Ltd.
First published in Great Britain in 2014 by
Andersen Press Ltd., 20 Vauxhall Bridge Road, London SW1V 2SA.
Published in Australia by Random House Australia Pty.,
Level 3, 100 Pacific Highway, North Sydney, NSW 2060.
Copyright © Chris Judge, 2014
The rights of Chris Judge to be identified as the author and illustrator
of this work have been asserted by him in accordance with the
Copyright, Designs and Patents Act, 1988.
All rights reserved. Printed and bound in Malaysia by Tien Wah Press.

1 3 5 7 9 10 8 6 4 2

British Library Cataloguing in Publication Data available.

ISBN 978 1 78344 163 1

TiN

CHRIS JUDGE

Andersen Press

Tin's mum asked him to look after his little sister, Nickel, for the afternoon.

"No problem," said Tin.

"Nickel, you play with your toys while I read my comic," said Tin, relaxing.

But the peace didn't last for long. "What's the matter, Zinc?" asked Tin.

"NICKEL!
How did you get up there so quickly?" yelled Tin in horror.

Tin jumped up the tree after Nickel.

Higher and higher they climbed...

...but just as Tin reached her...

She floated away!

Tin scrambled down the tree and leapt on to his bicycle.

Tin and Zinc chased Nickel all the way into the big city.

Tin cycled as fast as he could.

Round and round, and up and up.

"I've got you Nickel!" exclaimed Tin, bravely leaping into the air.

Tin, Nickel and Zinc slowly drifted
up over the city until, unfortunately,
the balloon burst.

POP!

"This is not good,"
he said.

"Oh dear," cried Tin,
as they plummeted
down through the air.

"Not good at all . . ."

Luckily, just at that moment . . .

...a big parade was passing beneath them.

Tin and Zinc landed with a BUMP on the back of a large, grey elephant.

While Nickel landed safely on the back of a long-necked giraffe.

But then all of the animals turned and marched into the Safari Park!

The elephant went one way . . .

. . . and the giraffe the other!

Tin and Zinc slid down the
elephant's trunk.

But Nickel was too quick
for them!

They raced across the shells of
three shocked tortoises.

Hurried past a daydreaming lion.

Ran between the legs of a
pink flamingo.

Through the mouth of a
surprised hippo.

Across the back of a strolling rhino.

Up and down a great big snake.

But Nickel wasn't quick enough to escape from the Safari Ranger.

"Oh Nickel, you gave us such a fright!" said Tin.

"I'm glad you are okay, but please don't do that again!" he said,
handing her a new balloon.

It was getting dark, so Tin retrieved his bicycle from the fairground and they all raced home before Mum noticed they were gone.